MW01027090

By Christy Webster

Illustrated by Meg Dunn

🌸 A GOLDEN BOOK • NEW YORK

CANDY LAND and HASBRO and all related trademarks and logos are trademarks of
Hasbro, Inc. © 2025 Hasbro. Published in the United States by Golden Books, an imprint of
Random House Children's Books, a division of Penguin Random House LLC, 1745 Broadway,
New York, NY 10019, and in Canada by Penguin Random House Canada Limited, Toronto.
Golden Books, A Golden Book, A Little Golden Book, the G colophon, and the distinctive
gold spine are registered trademarks of Penguin Random House LLC.
rhcbooks.com
ISBN 978-0-593-90066-6 (trade) — ISBN 978-0-593-90067-3 (ebook)
Printed in the United States of America
10 9 8 7 6 5 4 3 2 1

My friend and I couldn't believe it. We were in Candy Land! We were heading to Candy Castle, so we had a long journey ahead of us. I led the way first.

We had a decision to make right away. To the left was a rainbow-colored trail. To the right, a sign pointed toward the Gingerbread Plum Trees.

The rainbow looked pretty, but the plums
sounded delicious! We took a right.

GINGERBREAD
PLUM TREES

We arrived at Gingerbread Plum Grove. The deep **GREEN** leaves fluttered in the breeze and the juicy **PURPLE** plums shimmered in the sun.

"Try one!" said a friendly **GREEN** troll, hopping out from behind a tree.

It was Plumpy! He helped us pick some tasty plums.

Then it was my friend's turn to lead the way.

The land ahead was cool and WHITE. Soon we saw giant candy canes rising out of the ground. "Peppermint!" my friend cheered.

A tall woodsman stepped forward, dressed in **PINK** and **RED**. "Welcome to the Peppermint Forest!" he said. "I'm Mr. Mint. Watch this!"

He chopped down a peppermint stick and carved it into two little flutes.

Toot! Toot! They made a happy sound— and tasted great!

It was my turn again to choose which way to go. I saw two paths ahead. I picked the one called Gumdrop Pass.

Along the path, the Gumdrop Mountains rose higher and higher. Each was a different color—GREEN, **BLUE**, PINK, YELLOW, and PURPLE. But instead of snow, they were covered in sugar. It was a gumdrop dream!

As we walked back onto the rainbow path, I stepped on a YELLOW gumdrop, and my foot sank. We were stuck!

"Well, this is a sticky situation!" I told my friend.

"Lift your knees!" a voice called out. It was Jolly! He showed us how to step out of the gooey gumdrops. He was a gumdrop expert!

My friend led us to the next signpost. It pointed to the Peanut Brittle House. We saw that a little cottage made of peanut brittle sat on a hill, surrounded by peanut plants. I'd never seen so many peanuts!

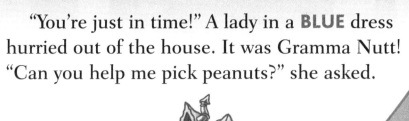

"You're just in time!" A lady in a **BLUE** dress hurried out of the house. It was Gramma Nutt! "Can you help me pick peanuts?" she asked.

We gladly helped Gramma Nutt. "Thank you!" she called as we left.

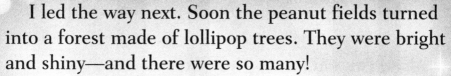

I led the way next. Soon the peanut fields turned into a forest made of lollipop trees. They were bright and shiny—and there were so many!

When I saw the same **RED** lollipop for the third time, I had to admit it: "I'm lost," I said.

Just then, someone twirled into view. "I love getting lost!" It was Princess Lolly!

"But how do you find your way?" I asked her.

"Follow your heart!" she said.

I looked ahead and saw a big **PURPLE** lollipop tree. It felt right. Sure enough, we found the path.

When my friend took his turn to lead, we found the shore of a strange sea. Instead of clear **BLUE** water, the waves were **PINK** and creamy— and ice cold!

"Welcome to the Ice Cream Sea!" The one and only Queen Frostine appeared from beneath the waves. The WHITE parts of her dress looked as sweet and fluffy as frosting on a birthday cake!

"You're almost to Candy Castle," she said. "Keep going!"

We hurried along the path and soon came to Molasses Swamp! The ground was covered with sticky, sweet **BROWN** molasses. It looked delicious, but it was hard to walk through. We got stuck again!

"Remember what Jolly said—lift your knees!" my friend called out.

"And what Princess Lolly said—follow your heart!" I said.

Slowly, we made our way through the swamp. We saw the castle in the distance!

Candy Castle looked like a bunch of giant ice-cream cones, with one scoop of every flavor! When we approached the door, we couldn't believe it—everyone we'd met along the way was there, plus King Candy!

"Welcome!" King Candy announced. "You're just in time for the Sweet Celebration—and you're the guests of honor!"

Our long journey was finally over. At the Sweet Celebration, we tried every treat. Then we danced with our new friends. Then, too soon, it was time to go home. But King Candy said we could come back anytime we wanted!

There's no place like Candy Land!